"Do you know why you came to my house today?" Casey asked.

"Um…no," said Marvin. He didn't want her to think he liked her.

"Because of this!" said Casey. She pulled something out of her pocket. "It's a magic crystal. It makes all your wishes come true." She showed it to Marvin.

Marvin took it from her and examined it. It was almost transparent, with flecks of green and gold.

"It used to be just a normal rock," Casey explained. "Then, last night, it got struck by lightning! And it turned into a magic crystal."

Books by Louis Sachar

The Marvin Redpost series

Sideways Stories from Wayside School

Wayside School Is Falling Down

Wayside School Gets a Little Stranger

Sideways Arithmetic from Wayside School

More Sideways Arithmetic from Wayside School

The Boy Who Lost His Face

Dogs Don't Tell Jokes

Holes

Johnny's in the Basement

Sixth Grade Secrets

Someday Angeline

There's a Boy in the Girls' Bathroom

Marvin Redpost

A Magic Crystal?

by Louis Sachar

illustrated by Amy Wummer

SCHOLASTIC INC.

New York Toronto London Auckland Sydney
Mexico City New Delhi Hong Kong Buenos Aires

To Sherre, Lucky, and Tippy

ISBN 0-439-10633-8

12 11 10 9 8 7 6 5 4 3 2 1   3 4 5 6 7 8/0

Printed in the U.S.A.   40

First Scholastic printing, March 2003

Contents

1. "Fight!"   1

2. The Old Fire Station   7

3. The Magic Crystal   16

4. The Wish   25

5. Two Wishes   35

6. Silence   47

7. A Conversation?   52

8. Last Chance   60

9. Her Sweet Voice   72

1

"Fight!"

School was over, but Marvin Redpost stayed in class. He needed to ask Mrs. North a question.

She was going through some papers. Marvin walked to her desk, then stared at her until she noticed him.

She turned to him and smiled. "Yes, Marvin?"

"Excuse me, Mrs. North," said Marvin. "When's the book report due?"

"I told you Tuesday," said Mrs. North.

Marvin nodded.

Mrs. North returned to her papers.

He still didn't know when the report was due. Did Mrs. North mean that it was due Tuesday? Or did she mean that she told him on Tuesday when it was due?

Mrs. North looked at Marvin again. She seemed surprised he was still there. "Do you have another question?" she asked.

He shook his head. He didn't have another question. He had the same question. He took his book and walked out of the classroom, then out of the building.

There was a great commotion out on the playground. A large group of kids had gathered near the swing set. Marvin could hear a lot of yelling. He heard someone shout, "Fight!"

He ran to see what was happening. When he reached the crowd, he could see two boys fighting on the sand, next to the swings. One of the fighters was Stuart Albright.

Stuart was Marvin's best friend.

Marvin pushed his way through the crowd to get a better look. The other fighter was Nick Tuffle.

Nick was also Marvin's best friend.

Marvin had two best friends. And they were rolling around on the ground, clawing and hitting each other.

"Get'm, Nick!" shouted Clarence.

"Kill him, Stuart!" yelled Travis.

"Rip his guts out!" screamed Heather.

"Tear his head off!" cried Gina.

Suddenly everyone stopped shouting as Mr. McCabe made his way through the crowd. Mr. McCabe was the principal.

Mr. McCabe didn't have to say anything.

Nick and Stuart stopped fighting. They untangled themselves from each other and stood up.

"I'm surprised at you, Stuart," said Mr. McCabe. "You too, Nick."

"Stuart started it!" said Nick. His face was red with anger.

"I did not," said Stuart. "You did!" The pocket on Stuart's shirt was torn. His glasses hung crooked on his face.

"You said I liked Casey Happleton!" said Nick.

Everybody laughed.

Except for Casey Happleton.

"That's because you said *I* liked Casey Happleton!" Stuart replied.

Everybody, except Casey, laughed again.

"You do!" said Nick.

"I do not!" said Stuart. "*You* do!"

"I hate her," said Nick.

"I hate her more than you!" said Stuart.

"No way!" said Nick.

"That's enough," said Mr. McCabe. "Now I want both of you to tell Casey you're sorry."

"What for?" asked Nick.

Mr. McCabe stared at him.

Nick looked down at the ground. "I'm sorry I hate you, Casey," he muttered.

"I don't care," said Casey. She had a ponytail that stuck out of the side of her head.

"I'm sorry I hate you, too," said Stuart.

"Whatever," said Casey.

Judy Jasper whispered something to Casey. Then the two girls laughed.

Mr. McCabe took Nick and Stuart to his

office. Everyone else started to leave, too.

Marvin didn't know what to do. He was supposed to go to Stuart's house after school today. But he knew Stuart wouldn't be going home for a very long time.

Someone tapped him on the shoulder. He turned around.

It was Casey Happleton.

"Do you want to come to my house, Marvin?" asked Casey.

"Okay."

2

The Old Fire Station

Marvin and Casey walked to the parking lot, where Casey's father was waiting for her. Marvin had never been to Casey's house before. He didn't know what to expect.

"I hope you like cats," said Casey.

"Oh, sure," said Marvin.

"You're not allergic?" Casey asked.

"I don't think so," said Marvin.

"That's good," said Casey.

"Do you have a lot of cats?" Marvin asked.

"No, I'm allergic," said Casey.

Casey's father waved to her from inside his car.

"This is Marvin Redpost," Casey told him. "He wants to come home with me."

"You do?" asked Casey's father.

Marvin blushed. "Well, she asked me," he said.

Casey got in the back seat and slid over to make room for Marvin. He sat down next to her.

Casey's father turned around and looked at Marvin. "So you're Marvin Redpost," he said. "Casey has told me a lot about you."

"I have not!" Casey insisted.

"Aren't you really a prince, who was kidnapped at birth?" asked her father.

"Yes, I mean no. I'm not really sure."

"He really likes cats a lot," said Casey.

"That's good," said Casey's father.

"But you don't have any cats," said Marvin, a little unsure.

"No, I hate the furry little things," said Casey's father.

Casey's sideways ponytail stuck out toward Marvin. It bounced up and down as the car drove over the speed bumps in the school parking lot.

"Do you know when the book report is due?" Marvin asked her.

"Yes," said Casey. "Mrs. North told us Tuesday."

Marvin nodded. He still didn't know what that meant.

"I'm going to have to call my mom when we get to your house," he said. "She thinks I'm at Stuart's."

"Do you know your phone number?" asked Casey.

"Of course," said Marvin. "Don't you?"

"No," said Casey.

That surprised Marvin. He'd known his phone number since kindergarten. "You should," he said.

"Why should I?" asked Casey.

"I don't know it either," said Casey's father from the front seat.

That *really* surprised Marvin. "Did you just move or something?" he asked.

"No," said Mr. Happleton.

They reached Casey's house. The house was four stories high. It had a very long driveway and a huge garage.

"I didn't know you lived in a mansion," Marvin said slowly.

"This house used to be a fire station,"

Mr. Happleton told him. "That was before Casey was born. The garage was even bigger than it is now. We remodeled. What's now the living room used to be part of the garage."

"Cool," said Marvin.

Mr. Happleton parked the car in the driveway. Marvin climbed out of the car.

"Don't forget your book," Casey reminded him.

Marvin's book lay on the back seat. He picked it up, then followed Casey into the house.

It looked pretty much like a normal house, except there was a pole right in the middle of the living room.

"That's the fire pole," said Casey. "The firemen used to slide down it when there was a fire."

"Cool," Marvin said as he walked over to it.

Marvin looked up. There was a round hole in the ceiling, and he could see another hole in the ceiling above that, and the one above that, too. The pole went all the way up to the fourth floor.

"Are you allowed to slide down it?" he asked.

"Sure," said Casey. "I do my homework at the very top. It's the library. Then, when my dad calls me to dinner, I slide down the pole."

"That is so cool," said Marvin.

"Here's the phone," said Casey's father, handing it to him.

Marvin set his book down on a table and took the phone. He called home. His mother seemed quite surprised when he told her he was at Casey Happleton's house.

"Can you give me their phone number?" she asked.

"No one knows it," said Marvin.

"What do you mean, no one knows it?"

Marvin put his hand next to his mouth and whispered into the phone. He didn't want to embarrass Casey and her father. "They don't know their own phone number."

"How could they not know their phone number?"

"I don't know."

"Let me speak to Casey's mother."

"Well, she might know it," said Marvin. "But she's not here. You can talk to her dad."

He handed the phone to Mr. Happleton. "My mom wants to talk to you."

To Marvin's surprise, he heard Mr. Happleton recite a phone number.

Marvin turned to Casey. "I thought your dad just said he didn't know your phone number."

"Are you crazy?" asked Casey. "Of course he knows our phone number!"

"Well, *you* don't," said Marvin.

"I do, too," said Casey. "I've known it since preschool."

Casey's father hung up the phone. He told Marvin his mother would come pick him up around five o'clock.

Marvin put up his hands. "Wait a minute. Didn't you both just tell me you didn't know your phone number?"

They looked at him strangely.

Marvin wondered if he was going crazy. "You asked me if I knew my phone number. I said I did, and then you both said you didn't."

"That's right," said Casey's father. "Why would I know your phone number? I just met you."

Marvin's book lay on the table. It was called *A Thousand Cats*.

3

The Magic Crystal

"Do you want to know a secret?" asked Casey.

Marvin shrugged.

"Follow me," she said. "I'll tell you in the library." She started up the stairs.

Marvin followed. He was glad to be going to the library. Maybe he'd get to slide down the fire pole.

By the time he reached the fourth floor, his legs were sore and he was out of breath. He was not used to climbing so many stairs.

"In here," said Casey.

She opened the door to the library. The room was shaped like an octagon. Every wall was covered with bookshelves. The fire pole came up through the middle of the room. There was a railing around it, so somebody wouldn't accidentally fall through the hole.

"Do you know why you came to my house today?" Casey asked him.

"Um…no," said Marvin. He didn't want her to think he liked her.

"Because of this!" said Casey. She pulled something out of her pocket. "It's a magic crystal. It makes all your wishes come true." She showed it to Marvin.

Marvin took it from her and examined it. It was almost transparent, with flecks of green and gold.

"It used to be just a normal rock," Casey explained. "Then, last night, it got struck by lightning! And it turned into a magic crystal."

Marvin remembered that it had stormed last night. The lightning and thunder had scared his little sister, Linzy. But how would Casey know that the lightning had struck this rock?

"I wished that you'd come to my house today," said Casey. "And here you are."

Marvin knew that had nothing to do with the rock. The only reason he was here was because Stuart and Nick had gotten into a fight. "What other wishes have you made?" he asked.

"Just two other wishes so far," said Casey. "You have to be real careful with wishes. First I wished that Judy and I would be friends forever."

That doesn't prove anything, Marvin thought.

"And then," said Casey, "remember when Clarence was bragging about how he can stick a needle through his finger?"

Marvin remembered. Clarence was grossing out everybody in class.

"I wished he'd be quiet," said Casey. "And he was!"

"Mrs. North told him to be quiet," Marvin pointed out.

"I wished it right before Mrs. North told him," said Casey.

Marvin didn't think that proved anything either.

"You try," said Casey.

Marvin looked at the rock.

"You have to close your eyes and squeeze the crystal as hard as you can, so that it hurts. Then make a wish," said Casey.

Marvin tried to think of something to wish for. He felt silly. He closed his eyes and squeezed the rock so hard it hurt the palm of his hand. "I wish I knew when the book report was due."

"That doesn't count," said Casey. "I already told you it was due Tuesday. You have to make a *real* wish."

"Okay," Marvin said, glad that he finally knew when the report was due. He closed his eyes and squeezed the rock again. "I wish I had an ice cream sundae."

He opened his eyes.

No ice cream sundae.

Casey leaned over the railing and screamed down into the hole. "Dad! Marvin wants an ice cream sundae!"

Marvin leaned over the railing as well. He saw Casey's father way down at the bottom of the pole. It was a long way down. Marvin wasn't so sure he wanted to slide down it anymore. He felt a little dizzy.

"How many scoops?" Casey's father called up.

"How many scoops do you want, Marvin?" Casey asked him.

"Uh, two."

"We both want two scoops!" Casey shouted.

She turned back to Marvin. "My dad makes the best ice cream sundaes."

"Well, that doesn't count," said Marvin. "If your dad makes it."

"Why not?" asked Casey. "You wished for an ice cream sundae. And now you're going to get one."

Still, it seemed to Marvin he would have gotten the sundae even without the magic crystal. But now that he thought about it, he did wonder why he'd agreed to come to Casey's house.

"When did you wish for me to come over?" he asked her. "Before or after Stuart and Nick got in a fight?"

"Before," said Casey.

"That's weird," said Marvin. "I was supposed to go to Stuart's house today. The only reason I didn't was because he had to stay after school for fighting."

Casey bit her finger.

The door to the library opened and a teenage girl came in.

"We're busy," said Casey.

"Oh, sorry," said the girl. "I didn't know you were in here." She looked at Marvin. "Is he your boyfriend?"

"No way!" Casey exclaimed. "He's just Marvin."

The girl looked at Marvin. "Marvin Redpost?" she asked.

Marvin wondered how she knew his last name.

The girl stared at Marvin. "Aren't you the boy who turned into a girl?"

"Uh…no," said Marvin. "I don't know what you're talking about."

"Oh," said the girl. "It must have been a different Marvin Redpost." She laughed, then turned and left the library.

"That's my sister, Tanya," said Casey. "She's just stupid."

A short while later, Mr. Happleton yelled up that the sundaes were ready.

"Let's go," said Casey. She ducked under the railing, grabbed the pole, then disappeared beneath the floor.

Marvin looked over the railing. His legs felt very weak. He took a long, deep breath.

He still held the magic crystal. He closed his eyes and whispered, "I wish I don't get hurt."

He ducked under the railing, took hold of the pole, and wrapped his legs around it. He let himself slide down, very, very slowly.

An elderly woman was watching television in the room just below the library. Tanya was there with her.

"Hi, Marvin," said Tanya. "This is my grandmother."

"Hi," he said, clutching the pole.

"Marvin?" asked Tanya's grandmother. "Aren't you the boy who picks his nose?"

Marvin slid beneath the floor.

4

The Wish

Marvin swallowed a spoonful of ice cream. The sundae was delicious. It might have been the best ice cream sundae he'd ever had in his whole life. It had burnt pecans and caramel sauce.

The crystal lay on the table between him and Casey.

Maybe there was something to this wish stuff after all, Marvin thought. So far, every wish had come true.

"Now what should we wish for?" he asked Casey. "How about a million dollars?"

Casey thought it over. "I'm not sure about that," she said.

"You're right," said Marvin. "*Two* million dollars."

"Ummm…that's kind of selfish, don't you think?" asked Casey.

Marvin felt hurt. He didn't think of himself as selfish. Besides, weren't wishes supposed to be selfish? Anyway, he didn't really believe it would come true.

Maybe that was the real reason Casey didn't want to wish for two million dollars, he thought. Maybe she only wanted to wish for things that had a chance of coming true. That way, she could still pretend to believe in the magic crystal.

"How about this?" he suggested. "Let's wish that nobody in Mrs. North's class is sick tomorrow."

"Good one!" Casey agreed.

He knew she'd like it. It wasn't selfish. But more important, it had a good chance of coming true.

"Hold out your hand," said Casey.

Marvin held out his right hand, palm up. Casey placed the magic crystal on top of his hand. Then she put her hand on top.

The rock was sandwiched between their two hands. The tips of their fingers pressed together.

"Close your eyes," she whispered.

Marvin closed his eyes, and they spoke together. "We wish nobody in Mrs. North's class is sick tomorrow."

More than anything, Marvin hoped it would come true.

*   *   *

The next morning, he walked to school with Nick and Stuart. Nick complained about how mean Mr. McCabe was, but he didn't really sound that mean to Marvin.

"So, what'd you do yesterday?" asked Stuart. "While we were stuck in Mr. McCabe's office."

"Just went over to someone's house," said Marvin.

"Whose house?" asked Nick.

"Just somebody's house," said Marvin.

He didn't dare tell them he went to Casey's house. They might think he liked her. They wouldn't understand about the magic crystal. Besides, he promised Casey not to tell anyone about it.

"Did you even know whose house it was?" asked Stuart. "Or did you just walk into some stranger's house?"

"It was an old fire station," said Marvin. "I got to slide down a fire pole."

"I thought you said it was a house," said Nick.

"It is. It used to be a fire station. Now it's a house. The fire pole is in the living room."

His friends looked at him oddly. He knew he wasn't making any sense. But at least they stopped asking whose house it was.

They got to school just as the first bell rang. Marvin hurried to class.

Casey Happleton was already at her desk.

"I hope no one's sick," Marvin said as he sat down next to her.

"They better not be," said Casey. "I'll kill anyone who's sick."

That was the only wish he and Casey had made. They agreed to make only one wish a day. Casey promised not to make any wishes by herself, without Marvin.

They watched the door. Marvin nodded and said "Good" to himself every time someone entered the room.

Kenny coughed.

Casey glared at him.

Kenny coughed again.

Casey went over to his desk. "Are you sick?" she asked.

"No, I don't think so," said Kenny.

"Then quit coughing!" Casey demanded.

Kenny didn't cough after that.

Casey returned to her seat. "He's not sick," she told Marvin.

Marvin wasn't worried about Kenny. He was worried about Gina and Clarence. Both of their desks were empty.

The second bell rang. Marvin glanced at Casey. She was frowning.

The principal's voice came over the P.A. system. Everyone stood for the Pledge of Allegiance.

Gina entered the classroom right after

the Pledge. "I'm sorry I'm late, Mrs. North," she said. "I didn't think I had to go to school today."

"Oh?" said Mrs. North. "And why was that, Gina?"

"I was sick last night. Really! I threw up twice and had a fever and everything! I was just going to lay in bed and watch cartoons today. But then, when my mom took my temperature this morning, I was all better. It's not fair!"

"That's too bad," agreed Mrs. North.

A big smile came across Marvin's face. "Did you hear that?" he whispered to Casey. "Gina was supposed to be sick today!"

"Big deal!" Casey grumbled. "What about Clarence?" She angrily hit her desk with both fists.

"Casey, is something the matter?" asked Mrs. North.

"No, nothing," muttered Casey.

"She's just worried about Clarence," said Marvin.

Mrs. North looked at Marvin oddly. "Casey is worried about Clarence?" she asked.

"Why isn't he here?" asked Casey.

Now Mrs. North looked oddly at Casey. "Clarence will be fine," she said. "His mother called the school this morning."

"Does he have a temperature?" asked Casey.

Again, Mrs. North looked oddly at Casey. She obviously had a hard time believing that Casey cared so much about Clarence.

"He stuck a needle through his thumb,

and it got infected," explained Mrs. North. "The doctor wants him—"

"Then he's not sick?" interrupted Casey.

"No, he's not sick," said Mrs. North.

"Yes!" shouted Casey. She jumped out of her seat and raised her arms in triumph.

Marvin smiled, too.

"I'm sure Clarence will appreciate your concern," said Mrs. North. "His thumb is badly swollen, and very sore. He can't even hold a pencil. Perhaps you should make him a get-well card, and let him know how much you care."

"I don't care if his thumb falls off!" Casey replied. "Just so long as he's not sick."

5

Two Wishes

Marvin hurried across the playground and got in line to play wall-ball. He was good at wall-ball. He usually won, but not all the time.

He hated to lose. He wasn't a bad sport. It was just that when he won, he got to keep playing. When he lost, he had to go to the end of the line. Wall-ball was a very popular game. Once he lost, he might not get a chance to play again.

He wondered if he could use the magic crystal to wish that he'd never lose again.

He doubted Casey would go along with it. Casey sometimes played wall-ball, too. Why would she wish for Marvin to always beat her?

Marvin didn't believe in the magic crystal. Not really. Still, he couldn't stop thinking about what Gina had said. *She was supposed to be sick today. She threw up twice!*

Nick and Stuart got in line behind Marvin.

"So, is it true?" asked Nick.

"I can't believe it," said Stuart.

Marvin wondered how they found out about the magic crystal. Maybe Casey told Judy, and Judy told Stuart.

"Is what true?" he asked.

"Did you go to Casey's house yesterday?" asked Stuart.

"Is she your girlfriend?" asked Nick.

"No," said Marvin. "I went to her house, but she isn't my girlfriend. I don't even like her."

"Then why'd you go to her house?" asked Stuart.

"You said you went to a fire station," said Nick.

"She lives in an old fire station," said Marvin. "That's why I went there. I wanted to slide down the fire pole."

His friends nodded. That seemed to make sense to them. Marvin knew they'd like to slide down a fire pole, too.

"Are you going to her house again today?" asked Nick.

"No way!" Marvin insisted.

Just then, Casey Happleton came walking toward them. The boys stopped talking and stared at her.

"Hi, Marvin," Casey said. "I'll see you after school today."

Marvin felt his cheeks redden.

Casey skipped away. Her ponytail bounced up and down.

"I'm not going to her house," Marvin explained. "She's coming to my house."

After school, Casey walked home with Marvin. He knew that Nick and Stuart were following them, making stupid jokes and laughing. He knew what they were thinking, but it wasn't true. She wasn't his girlfriend. He didn't even like her.

Casey talked nonstop the whole way home. She talked about Clarence's fat thumb, and Gina throwing up, and her favorite cartoon shows, and wall-ball, and a million other things.

Casey was funny, but Marvin tried not to laugh. He knew Nick and Stuart were watching.

There was a white fence around the Redpost house, with one red post next to the gate. Marvin's father painted the red post once a year. Casey laughed when she saw it.

"A red post!" she said. "I get it."

"It's good luck," Marvin said. He tapped the red post as he walked through the gate.

Casey tapped it, too.

Marvin's little sister, Linzy, met them at the door. She stared at Casey a long time, then said, "Who are you?"

"I'm Casey," said Casey. "Who are you?"

Linzy didn't say anything.

"That's my sister, Linzy," said Marvin.

"Hi, Linzy," said Casey.

"You're a girl," said Linzy.

Casey turned to Marvin and said, "Your sister's really smart."

Marvin laughed.

"I know a boy named Casey," Linzy said. "He's in my kindergarten."

"I used to be a boy," said Casey. "I kissed my elbow and turned into a girl."

Linzy giggled. "Your ponytail sticks out of the side of your head," she said.

"Yes, it does," said Casey.

"It's supposed to stick out the back," said Linzy.

"Really?" asked Casey.

"Yes," said Linzy. "You don't know that, because you used to be a boy."

"Thanks, Linzy. I'll try to remember that," said Casey.

"If you want to know anything else about being a girl, just ask me," said Linzy. "I've been a girl my whole life."

Marvin's mother came out of her office. "Would you and your friend like a snack?" she asked. "I made chocolate-chip cookies."

Marvin wanted to tell his mother that Casey wasn't his friend, but he thought that might be rude.

"Sure," he said with a shrug.

"Thank you, Mrs. Redpost," Casey said politely.

Marvin started to follow his mother into the kitchen, but Casey grabbed his arm, stopping him. She had a gleam in her eye. She showed Marvin the magic crystal and whispered, "I wished for homemade cookies!"

Marvin felt very happy sitting next to Casey, eating homemade cookies. The cookies seemed to taste especially good because Casey had wished for them.

But then he thought about it. How did

he know Casey really wished for cookies? When did she wish for the cookies? Hadn't they agreed they'd make all their wishes together? And only one wish a day?

Either Casey lied when she said she wished for the cookies. Or she could have made a lot of secret wishes, and only told him about the ones that came true.

The cookies didn't taste so great anymore.

"This is so cool, Marvin!" said Casey. "We can wish for anything in the whole world! What do you want to wish for?"

"I don't care," Marvin grumbled.

"What's wrong?" asked Casey.

Marvin shrugged and said, "Nothing."

"What's the matter?" asked Casey.

"You promised not to make any wishes without me," Marvin said.

"I didn't," said Casey.

"What about the cookies?" said Marvin.

"Oh, that doesn't count," said Casey. "It was just a little wish. It wasn't a big wish."

"How many other little wishes did you make?" asked Marvin.

"That's the only one. I promise." She crossed her heart.

Marvin didn't know if he could believe her.

"You don't believe me, do you?" she asked.

"It doesn't matter," said Marvin.

"Here," said Casey. She handed Marvin the crystal. "You make a wish all by yourself. Wish for anything you want."

Marvin took the rock, but he really didn't feel like making his own wish. The fun part was making wishes together.

"If you're mad that I wished for cookies, then you wish for something."

"I'm not mad," said Marvin.

"I didn't get mad when you wished for an ice cream sundae," said Casey.

"I'm not mad," Marvin said again, although he was beginning to get a little angry.

"You're eating the cookies, too," Casey pointed out.

"I know," said Marvin.

"Just wish for something!" said Casey. "Whatever you want. Wish for a million dollars, Marvin. You can keep it all yourself. You don't have to give any to me, even though I'm sharing *my* cookies with you."

"They're not *your* cookies," said Marvin.

Casey pushed the plate away. "Oh, now I can't have a cookie!" she snapped.

"That's not what I meant," said Marvin.

"First you say I can have a cookie," Casey complained. "Then you say I can't. Then you say I can. Then you say I can't. Then you say I can. Then you say I can't."

Marvin closed his eyes.

"Just make a stupid wish, Marvin!" Casey demanded.

"I wish you'd shut up!"

6

Silence

Casey didn't say anything for the next five minutes, which had to be a record for her.

Marvin felt bad for telling her to shut up. He felt bad for having made such a big deal over her cookie wish.

He tried to pretend there was nothing wrong. He bit into a cookie. "Ummm, good cookie!" he said enthusiastically. "I'm sure glad you wished for these."

Casey didn't say anything.

"So, what should we wish for?" he asked.

Casey didn't say anything. She took the crystal from Marvin and put it in her pocket.

"Are you mad at me?" Marvin asked her.

Casey shook her head.

"Then why won't you say anything?"

Casey smiled at him.

"Oh, I get it," said Marvin. "Because I wished you'd shut up, now you're pretending you can't talk."

Casey didn't say anything.

"I know you're just pretending," said Marvin. "I know you can talk if you want to."

Casey just smiled.

"Besides," said Marvin, "don't you remember? You told me you wished Clarence would stop talking. He can still talk."

Casey rubbed her chin. She looked sideways at Marvin.

He knew what she was thinking. She was thinking that she had wished Clarence would stop talking about sticking a needle through his thumb. That was different. Marvin had wished for a total "shut up."

"I don't see the difference," Marvin said.

Casey glanced at him in a way that seemed to say, *I can't help it if you're stupid.*

"You're faking," Marvin accused.

Casey shrugged.

"Well, what do you want to do then?" Marvin asked. "You want to watch TV? You don't have to talk to do that."

Casey shrugged.

"All right, let's watch TV," said Marvin. "*Teenage Caveman* is on. Let's see if you can watch that without laughing."

Casey shrugged.

Teenage Caveman was one of Marvin's favorite shows. He knew Casey liked it, too. She could imitate the teenage caveman's voice perfectly. She always made him laugh.

Casey followed Marvin into the family room. He turned on the TV.

Casey watched the entire show without laughing or saying one word.

Marvin didn't laugh either. The show didn't seem as funny as usual.

Casey's father came by at five o'clock to take Casey home.

"It was very nice to get to meet you, Casey," said Marvin's mother.

"Bye, Casey," shouted Linzy.

Casey smiled at Marvin's mother and waved to Linzy.

After she left, Marvin's mother told him that Casey seemed like a very nice girl. "Although she's kind of quiet, isn't she?"

Marvin didn't say anything.

7

A Conversation?

Casey could talk. Marvin was sure of it. If she couldn't talk, one of her parents would have called and asked what happened.

He knew she'd have to say something in school. It would be impossible for her to go through a whole day in school without saying one word.

"Good morning, Casey," he said as he sat down next to her.

She smiled at him, but said nothing.

He watched her during the Pledge of

Allegiance. Her mouth formed the words, but she didn't speak.

Finally, during math, Mrs. North asked her a question.

Casey pointed to her mouth. Then she held her hands out, as if to say she was helpless.

"She can't talk," said Judy Jasper.

"Do you have laryngitis?" asked Mrs. North.

Casey shrugged.

Marvin knew Casey didn't have laryngitis. When you have laryngitis, you can still speak in a sort of raspy whisper. Casey had faker-itis!

Mrs. North had Casey come to the front of the room and write the problem, and answer, on the board.

"Very good, Casey," Mrs. North said

when Casey finished. "I hope you feel better soon. Although I must say, I had been wondering why it was so nice and quiet in here this morning."

Several kids laughed.

Casey smiled at Mrs. North. Then she turned and stared angrily at Marvin.

Marvin stared right back at her. He knew she would have to talk sooner or later. He doubted she could make it to recess.

Casey made it to recess.

Marvin stared at her from the wall-ball line. She was standing on the blacktop with Judy and Melanie. Suddenly, Judy and Melanie laughed.

Marvin grabbed Stuart's arm. "She said something," he announced.

"Who?" asked Stuart.

"Why else would they laugh?" asked Marvin. "If she didn't say anything?"

"Who?" asked Nick.

She probably said something about me, Marvin thought. *Judy and Melanie are laughing at me.* He felt his ears get hot.

A ball hit Marvin's shoulder. He quickly spun around.

"You're up, Marvin," said Travis.

He'd been waiting all recess for his turn. But now he just walked away and said, "I have to talk to Casey."

"But she can't talk," Stuart called after him.

Casey had her back to Marvin, but turned around as he approached. She stared at him, hands on hips. Melanie and Judy backed off.

Marvin marched right up to her. "What

did you say about me?" he demanded.

Casey's eyes widened.

Marvin could tell what she was thinking. He could read her face. Her face said, *How can I say something about you? I can't talk. Remember?*

"Don't give me that," said Marvin. "I saw Judy and Melanie laugh."

Casey's face said, *So? They're allowed to laugh. It's a free country.*

"You're going to get into trouble when Mrs. North finds out you don't have laryngitis," said Marvin.

Casey held out her hands. *It's not my fault I can't talk.*

"First of all," said Marvin, "I don't believe in your stupid magic crystal. It's not even a crystal. It's just a rock. How do you know it got struck by lightning? And besides, you're the one who has it. If it really is magical, all you have to do is wish that you can talk again."

Casey raised her eyebrows. Her eyebrows seemed to say, *How can I make a wish if I can't talk?*

"Oh, yeah," said Marvin. He hadn't thought of that. "All right. Give me the rock, and I'll wish that you can talk again."

Casey looked at him.

Marvin wasn't quite sure what her face said. It either said, *You just said you don't believe in the rock. It won't work if you don't believe.*

Or else it said, *No way! I can't trust you, Marvin. Not after your last wish.*

"Well, then, give the rock to Judy and let her wish for you," said Marvin.

Casey puffed out her cheek with her

tongue. This seemed to say, *Judy doesn't know about the magic crystal. She doesn't know that's why I can't talk. And since I can't talk, I can't tell her.*

"Well, write it all down on paper for her," said Marvin.

Yeah, right! answered Casey's angry face. *You know I hate to write. It's bad enough I have to write for school. If I tried to write all that to Judy, it would take ten sheets of paper. And I'd probably sprain my hand.*

"Now you're exaggerating," Marvin said.

Are you insane? asked Casey's scrunched-up nose.

"You're just being stubborn," Marvin replied.

Casey's face turned red. *I'm stubborn? You're the one who's stubborn! You're a stupid, stinky booboo-head baboon!*

"Fine, be that way!" said Marvin. "I don't care if you never talk again!" He turned his back on her and angrily walked away.

The bell rang before he made it back to the wall-ball area. Now he was really mad. He'd wasted his entire recess, and it was all Casey's fault!

He used to kind of like her. Sort of. But not anymore! Not after she called him a stupid, stinky booboo-head baboon!

8

Last Chance

Casey did not say a word all day. At least not when Marvin was near. He didn't know if she said anything when he wasn't around, although he suspected that she did.

After school, he walked with Nick and Stuart to Nick's house. "She's lying," Marvin repeated several times on the way there.

"How can she lie if she can't talk?" asked Stuart.

"That's how," said Marvin. "Because she *can* talk."

"Why would she pretend she can't talk?" asked Nick.

"Why do you care?" asked Stuart.

"I don't care!" Marvin insisted.

He didn't tell them about the magic crystal. He had promised Casey to keep it secret. And even though she was pretending she couldn't talk, and even though she called him a stupid, stinky booboo-head baboon, he still kept his promise.

"You want to play basketball?" Nick asked when they reached his house.

"I don't care," Marvin repeated, still thinking about Casey.

"Sure," said Stuart. "Horse, or knock-out?"

"I don't care," said Marvin. "I just know she's faking."

They decided to play horse, because they'd need two basketballs to play knockout. Nick only had one basketball.

Nick talked and played at the same time. "…Yes, ladies and gentlemen. The amazing Nick Tuffle is now going to try a shot from behind the brown spot in the driveway! Can he do it? He's taking careful aim. Oh, the pressure! It would be amazing if he can make this shot. He shoots! The ball is up. It bounces off the rim…and GOES THROUGH THE NET! He did it! Nick Tuffle made the shot!"

Marvin was the first to lose. He was too busy thinking about how much he didn't care about Casey.

"Why don't you go home and get your basketball?" Stuart said. "Then we can play knockout."

Marvin liked knockout better than horse. It was faster and had a lot more action.

He only lived around the block from Nick. He headed home.

His basketball was kept in the garage, but the garage door was closed, so he had to go through the house.

Jacob and Nate were eating popcorn in the kitchen. Jacob was Marvin's older brother. Nate was Jacob's best friend. They were in middle school.

They were two-fisted eaters. Sometimes all four fists were in the large popcorn bowl at the same time.

"Hey, Mar," said Jacob. "You have a visitor."

"I do?" asked Marvin.

"Is she your girlfriend?" asked Nate.

"My girlfriend?" asked Marvin.

"She's cute," said Jacob.

"Who are you talking about?" asked Marvin.

"You mean there's more than one?" asked Nate.

Nate and Jacob laughed.

"How many girlfriends do you have?" asked Jacob.

They laughed some more.

Marvin felt himself blush. "I don't know who you're talking about. And she's *not* my girlfriend!"

"She's upstairs, playing with Linzy," said Jacob.

Marvin rushed up the stairs.

"He's sure in a hurry to see her!" said Nate.

Marvin stopped. The only reason he was hurrying was because Nick and Stuart were waiting for him. He probably shouldn't even go upstairs at all. He should just get his basketball and leave.

But maybe he could catch Casey talking.

Very quietly, he continued up the stairs, then down the hall to Linzy's room.

The door was open. He peeked inside.

Casey and Linzy were sitting on the floor, playing Candy Land. Casey's back was to Marvin. Marvin put his fingers to his lips so Linzy wouldn't say anything.

"Hi, Marvin!" Linzy blurted. "Do you like my new hairstyle?"

Linzy had a ponytail sticking out of the side of her head.

Casey turned and stared at Marvin.

"I'm playing with Casey," Linzy said. "She can't talk. And it's your fault."

Marvin spoke to Linzy, but he looked at Casey. "How do you know she can't talk?" he asked. "Unless she *told* you."

"Well…because she hasn't said anything!" said Linzy.

"But how do you know it's my fault?"
Marvin asked, still staring at Casey.

Everything is your fault, Marvin, said
Casey's face.

"Well, you two have fun playing Candy

Land," said Marvin. "I just came to get my basketball."

"Wait! Don't go!" said Linzy. "You can fix her so she can talk again."

"Oh, really?" asked Marvin. "How can I do that?"

"All you have to do is say you're sorry for telling her to shut up," said Linzy.

Marvin thought it over. He did feel bad about telling Casey to shut up.

Casey tapped Linzy's shoulder.

"Oh, I forgot," said Linzy. She giggled. "You also have to say that you 'miss hearing her sweet voice.'" She giggled again.

Marvin reddened. There was no way he could say *that!*

"Well, first of all," said Marvin, "I know she's faking. Second of all, what makes you think I want her to talk again? I'm going to play basketball. Nick and Stuart are waiting for me."

Casey glared at him. Her face said, *If you leave now, you'll be really, really sorry!*

He turned and went down the stairs. He got his basketball out of the garage and headed back to Nick's house.

The whole way there, Marvin thought about Casey. There was no way he would tell her he "missed hearing her sweet voice." He was willing to say he was sorry. If that wasn't good enough, well, too bad!

"What took you so long?" Stuart asked when Marvin finally made it back to Nick's house.

"C'mon, let's play knockout," said Nick.

Marvin looked at his basketball. He suddenly realized something. How could

Linzy know he had to say he "missed hearing her sweet voice" unless Casey told her?

Casey couldn't have written it for her, because Linzy couldn't read! That proved it. Casey must have talked.

"I have to go home," he said.

"But you just got here," said Stuart.

"I got stuff I have to do," Marvin said.

"What kind of stuff?" asked Nick.

"Just stuff," said Marvin. He couldn't tell them about Casey being at his house. They wouldn't understand. They might think he liked her.

He turned and hurried home.

He tapped the red post for luck, then went inside.

Linzy, Jacob, and Nate were playing cards on the floor of the family room. That

surprised Marvin almost as much as seeing Casey earlier. Jacob and Nate never played with Linzy.

"Nate, do you have any sevens?" Linzy asked.

"Hey, Mar," said Jacob.

Linzy laughed as Nate angrily threw a card at her.

"Where's Casey?" Marvin asked.

"Your girlfriend went home," said Nate.

"She's not my girlfriend," said Marvin.

"She's really, really mad at you," said Linzy.

Marvin shrugged. "I don't care."

"She hates you," said Linzy.

"So?" said Marvin.

He took his basketball through the laundry room and out to the garage. He tossed it into the ball box, but it bounced out and hit his bicycle, which crashed to the ground.

Marvin grumbled, then picked up his bike. He looked around for the basketball. It had rolled under the van.

He got a broom off the wall, then lay down on the floor of the garage. Using the broomstick, he knocked the ball out from under the van.

"I hate her, too," he said.

9

Her Sweet Voice

Marvin tried to read his book, *A Thousand Cats,* but couldn't concentrate. He kept glancing at Casey.

It was Friday, two days since he wished she would shut up. She still wasn't talking. He wondered how long she could go on pretending.

Casey caught him looking at her. She glared back at him, as if to say, *What are you looking at?*

Marvin didn't look away. *You're going to have to talk sometime,* he thought. *You can't keep this up forever.*

That's what you think! replied Casey's face.

You'll get in trouble, thought Marvin. *Mrs. North will find out you don't have laryngitis!*

I may never talk again, Casey shot back.

Good! thought Marvin. *I'm sick of hearing your ugly voice.*

Well, I'm sick of your stupid, ugly face! Casey silently replied.

And I'm sick of your stupid, ugly ponytail! thought Marvin.

Casey angrily turned away.

Marvin looked down at his desk. Even though he was mad at Casey, he felt bad about what he had just said. He knew she was very proud of her ponytail.

"You are all working so nice and quietly," said Mrs. North. She dropped three marbles into the marble jar, filling it to the top. "Let's go to Lake Park!"

Everybody cheered—except Casey, who couldn't, and Marvin, who didn't feel very cheerful.

Lake Park was three blocks from Marvin's school. Everyone had to walk with a buddy. Marvin's buddy was Stuart. Nick and Warren walked right behind them.

"Look, there's Casey," Marvin said. "Watch. I bet you she'll talk."

Casey was buddies with Judy.

"I don't care," said Stuart.

"I don't care either," said Marvin.

Mrs. North started out at the front, but then she drifted back until she was walking next to Judy and Casey.

"Darn!" said Marvin. "Now she won't say anything with Mrs. North right there."

"I don't care," said Stuart.

"Me neither," said Marvin.

"I hope it's all right for you to be outside," he heard Mrs. North say. "I wouldn't want your throat to get worse."

Casey shrugged.

"The fresh air will be good for her," said Judy.

Marvin turned to Stuart. "How does Judy know?" he asked. "Is she a doctor?"

"Who cares?" asked Stuart.

"Not me," said Marvin.

There was a big playscape at Lake Park and a huge spider web made out of rope, which was fun to climb.

Mrs. North told the class to have fun.

Marvin didn't feel like having fun. He watched Casey and Judy walk down the path to the lake.

"C'mon, Marvin!" Stuart called as he ran to the spider web.

Marvin stayed behind. He knew Casey and Judy were going off by themselves so they could talk. This was his chance to catch her. He waited for them to get a head start, then followed them.

There were lots of trees on either side of the path. Marvin crept quietly from tree to tree.

The two girls stopped near the edge of the lake. Marvin remained behind a tree. It looked as if they were talking, but Casey had her back to him. He was still too far away to hear.

He moved closer.

He heard a laugh. He didn't know if it came from Judy or Casey, but either way it proved Casey could talk. If Judy was the one who laughed, it meant that Casey must have said something funny.

He carefully moved to a closer tree, then quickly darted to a bush, less than ten feet away from the girls. He tried not to breathe.

"*Sh!*" said Judy. "I think I hear someone."

Marvin remained very still.

"We know you're there, Marvin!" said Judy.

For a moment, Marvin didn't say anything. Then he stepped out from behind the bush.

"I heard you!" he declared. "Casey talked."

"No she didn't," Judy insisted.

Casey pointed to her mouth, which was zipped shut.

"What did she say?" demanded Judy.

Marvin bit his lip. He wished he had

heard just a little bit more. "I heard some-one laugh," he said.

"That was me," said Judy.

"Well, she must have said something funny, to make you laugh," said Marvin.

"She made a funny face," said Judy.

Casey demonstrated. She pulled her ears, raised her eyebrows, and stuck her tongue out of the side of her mouth.

Marvin suddenly realized something. "You said, *'Sh!'* to her."

"Huh?" asked Judy.

"When you heard me behind the bush. You said, *'Sh!* I think I hear someone.' You wouldn't have said, *'Sh!'* unless Casey could talk."

He smiled triumphantly at Casey.

"I was talking about *sh*oes," Judy

explained. "I was just about to say, 'Shoes are nice,' when I heard you sneaking around like a skunk."

Casey smiled triumphantly at Marvin.

"Marvin!" shouted Mrs. North from the top of the path. "Judy! Casey! Come back to the playscape. You're not allowed near the water."

Judy hurried away before Marvin could ask her why she was talking about shoes.

Casey looked at Marvin. Her face wasn't angry. He wasn't sure what her face was saying.

Marvin sighed. "Okay," he said. "I'm sorry I told you to shut up."

Casey waited for more.

Marvin shook his head. "Okay. Okay," he said. He looked around to make sure nobody could hear him. He stared down at his feet and muttered, "I miss hearing your sweet voice."

He glanced up at her.

She removed the magic crystal from her pocket and held it out to him.

Marvin took it. He closed his eyes and said, "I wish you can talk again."

He opened his eyes.

Casey spoke. She said, "You're weird, Marvin!"

Then she ran up the path, screaming at the top of her lungs. "HEY, MRS. NORTH! I GOT MY VOICE BACK! IT'S A MIRACLE!"

Marvin stayed behind, still holding the magic crystal. He closed his eyes. He squeezed it so hard it hurt his hand. Then he whispered, "I wish, someday, Casey and I will get married."

He threw the rock as far as he could, out over the lake.

Marvin Redpost #1:
Kidnapped at Birth?

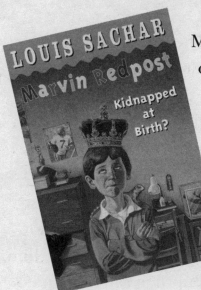

Marvin suddenly figures out why he has red hair and blue eyes, while the rest of his family has *brown* hair and *brown* eyes. He's not really Marvin Redpost at all. He is Robert, the lost prince of Shampoon!

"Wonderfully logical and absurd, with wit and attention to detail rare in an easy reader… Aside from being resoundingly funny, Sachar has a rare honesty about what children really encounter in the world."
—*The Bulletin of the Center for Children's Books*

"My name's not Marvin."
—Marvin Redpost

Marvin Redpost #2:
Why Pick on Me?

The rumor is going around that Marvin is the biggest nose-picker in the school. Now everyone is acting as if the rumor is true! Even Marvin's best friends don't want to be seen with him. But what can Marvin do about it?

"Vintage Sachar—ingenious, funny, gross—
and with a believable resolution."
—*Kirkus Reviews*

"Marvin's the biggest nose-picker
in the whole school."
—Melanie, Marvin's classmate

Marvin Redpost #3:
Is He a Girl?

Everyone knows that if a boy kisses his elbow, he'll turn into a girl. So when Marvin's lips touch his elbow, he's not surprised that he starts acting strange—like wishing he had pigtails and wanting to play hopscotch. He's even started dotting his *i*'s with little hearts! Will Marvin *ever* return to normal?

"Sachar writes for beginning readers with a comic simplicity that is never banal."
—*Booklist*

"There's nothing Marvin Redpost can't do."
—Stuart Albright, Marvin's best friend

Marvin Redpost #4:
Alone in His Teacher's House

Marvin's friends think he's the luckiest boy in the world when Mrs. North asks him to dog-sit for a week. He gets $3 a day, plus a $4 bonus if nothing goes wrong. And he gets to be alone in Mrs. North's house! But pretty soon it starts to look as if Marvin *won't* be getting that bonus after all...

"Sachar's finely tuned sense of how children think and feel makes this fourth book about Marvin and his comic misadventures entertaining."
—*The Horn Book*

"Marvin's going to use the bathroom in Mrs. North's house!"
—Melanie, Marvin's classmate

Marvin Redpost #5:
Class President

It's "Hole Day" at school, and even Mrs. North and Principal McCabe are wearing their worst clothes. But now they're expecting company—the President of the United States is on his way! And there's no time to change!

"The story hums along with its own cheerful energy, much like Marvin himself."
—*Kirkus Reviews*

"Good job, Marvin."
—the President

Marvin Redpost #6:
A Flying Birthday Cake?

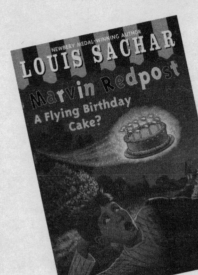

Marvin can't sleep. Suddenly something zooms across the sky. It looks a lot like Nick's birthday cake! Could it be? Or is it something else? The next day there's a new boy in school. His name is Joe Normal, but everyone thinks he's weird. What is *normal,* anyway? Certainly not a flying birthday cake!

★ "A smart, funny twist on the new-kid theme."
—*The Horn Book* (starred review)

"His name should be Marvin Stupid."
—Casey Happleton, Marvin's friend?

Marvin Redpost #7:
Super Fast, Out of Control!

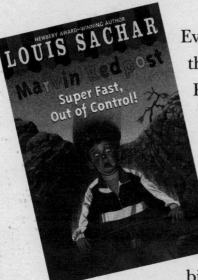

Everyone at school thinks that Marvin Redpost is going to ride his new bike down Suicide Hill. But not only is Marvin terrified of the steep hill, he's afraid of his new bike! How can Marvin survive this one?

"If Marvin says he'll ride down Suicide Hill,
then he'll ride down Suicide Hill."
—Stuart Albright, Marvin's best friend